Detective Pony

Do you love ponies? Be a Pony Pal!

Look for these Pony Pal books:

PONY PALS

Detective Pony

Jeanne Betancourt

Illustrated by Paul Bachem

A
LITTLE APPLE
PAPERBACK

SCHOLASTIC INC.
New York Toronto London Auckland Sydney

ISBN 0-590-37460-5

12 11 10 9 8 7 6 5 4   8 9/9 0 1 2/0

Printed in the U.S.A.   40

First Scholastic printing, January 1998

This Pony Pal book is for Lee Minoff.

Thank you to Dr. Kent Kay, Linda Brink, and volunteer firefighter Bridgitte Ruthman.

Contents

Detective Pony

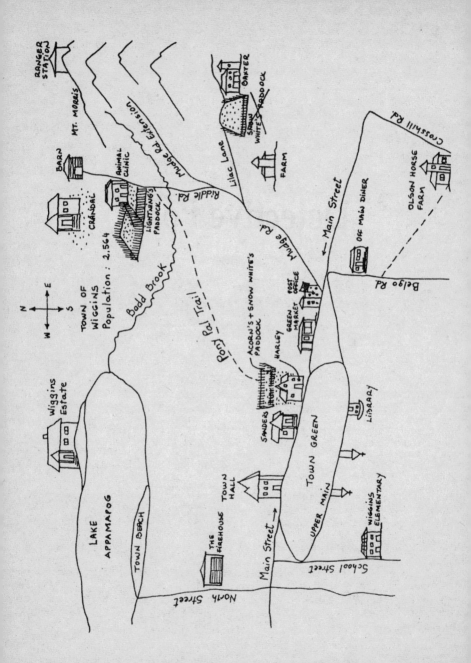

A Visitor

Anna Harley came out her back door and ran across the backyard. There were two ponies in the paddock behind Anna's house and yard. "Hey, ponies," Anna called out. "We're going for a trail ride."

Anna's pony, Acorn, was standing in the pony shed. The other pony, Snow White, belonged to Anna's next-door neighbor and Pony Pal, Lulu Sanders.

Snow White came over to Anna, but Acorn stayed in the shed. Anna thought that Acorn was trying to hide from her. He liked to play Catch Me if You Can.

Anna went into the shed. Acorn wasn't playing. He was staring at a fluffy black cat with white paws sitting on a bale of straw. The cat was staring back at Acorn.

"Hey, kitty," said Anna. "What are you doing here?"

Lulu came into the shed behind Anna. "Whose cat is that?" she asked.

"I don't know," answered Anna. "I've never seen him before."

Suddenly a mouse ran from behind the feed bin. The cat jumped to the ground and chased the mouse out of the shed. Acorn nickered as if to say, "Good work!"

The cat leaped back up on the straw and curled himself into a ball. Acorn took a few steps toward the cat and sniffed him. The cat purred. Acorn nickered softly.

"That's so cute!" said Lulu.

Pam Crandal rode her pony, Lightning, up to the shed. She said hi to her Pony Pals and dismounted.

Anna pointed at the cat. "Acorn has a new friend," she said.

"But we don't know where he comes from or who owns him," said Lulu. "Do you?"

Pam picked up the cat and looked him over. "I've never seen him before," she said.

"Do you think he's a stray?" asked Anna.

"He doesn't have a collar," said Pam. "But some people don't put collars on their cats."

"We should make a poster saying we found him," said Anna. "Just in case someone lost him."

"Maybe he's not lost," said Lulu. "Maybe he lives around here and he's just visiting."

"Let's go for a trail ride," said Pam. "If he's still here when we come back we'll make a poster."

Anna and Lulu agreed with Pam. They saddled up their ponies and mounted. The cat watched.

"Bye, kitty," said Anna. "It's time for you to go home."

The Pony Pals rode across the paddock onto Pony Pal Trail. The mile-and-a-half trail went from the Crandals' fields to Acorn and Snow White's paddock. Anna and her pals loved riding on Pony Pal Trail. "No school for a whole week," Anna shouted. "I love vacations."

"We're going to have so much fun!" Pam said.

"Look, Anna," Lulu called. "The cat is following us."

Anna turned and saw the cat running along the trail behind them. Acorn saw him, too. He nickered happily.

When the ponies galloped along a straight stretch of trail, the cat ran beside Acorn. Anna slowed Acorn to a halt at three birch trees. The cat ran up one of the trees and sat on a limb near Acorn's face. Pam and Lulu pulled up beside Anna.

"This cat really likes Acorn," said Anna.

"Maybe we should bring the cat to your father," said Lulu. "He might know who owns him."

"Good idea," said Anna.

Pam's father was a veterinarian and he took care of most of the cats, dogs, horses, cows, and pigs in Wiggins.

"He has office hours this morning," said Pam. "So we should go right now."

The cat followed the Pony Pals to the animal clinic. They put their ponies in the paddock next to the Crandals' new barn. Anna picked up the cat, and the three girls went into the clinic waiting room.

A man sat in one of the orange plastic chairs. A German shepherd dog sat at his feet. Pam patted the German shepherd's head. "How you doing, Brandy?" she asked the dog. Brandy sniffed Pam's hand.

"He's having an operation today," the man told Pam. "He has to stay overnight in the kennel room."

Dr. Crandal came to the door of the waiting area. He was surprised to see the Pony Pals there. Pam told him how they found the cat.

Brandy rubbed against Dr. Crandal's leg. "I'll look at the cat after I put Brandy in the kennel," said Dr. Crandal.

The man and Brandy followed Dr. Crandal into the back of the clinic.

A few minutes later the Pony Pals were in Dr. Crandal's examining room. He put the cat on the examining table and looked him over.

"I've never seen this cat," Dr. Crandal said. "But I can tell you he hasn't lived outdoors all his life. He doesn't have any scars and has eaten well. He's also been altered. Someone definitely took care of him." Dr. Crandal listened to the cat's heart and lungs with his stethoscope. "Good heart and lungs," he said. He handed the cat back to Anna. "I'm going to give him a booster shot, just in case he's missed some shots." He opened a drawer and took out a needle. Anna held the cat while Dr. Crandal gave him the shot.

"We're going to make posters about the cat," Anna told him. "In case someone in Wiggins lost him."

"Good idea," said Dr. Crandal. "He can sleep in the kennel tonight. I have room."

"Thanks, Dr. Crandal," said Lulu.

The Pony Pals said good-bye to Dr. Crandal and brought the cat back outside. Anna put him on the ground. The cat scooted under the paddock fence and over to Acorn. Acorn nickered happily.

"That is such a perfect cat," said Anna. "I wish Acorn and I could have him."

"Maybe nobody will claim him," said Pam. "Then you could keep him."

"That would be so much fun," said Lulu.

"I can't have a cat," said Anna sadly. "My mother sneezes and breaks out in big red spots when she's near a cat. She's allergic to them."

"Too bad," said Lulu. "He's such a nice cat."

"I hope someone claims him," said Pam.

The cat jumped up on the highest fence rail and sat on the post. Acorn and the cat sniffed each other's faces.

Anna wondered what would happen to Acorn's great new friend.

Screaming Ponies

The Pony Pals went into Pam's house to have a snack and to make posters about the cat. Pam put big pieces of paper, pencils, and Magic Markers on the kitchen table.

As Anna drew a picture of the black cat, she thought about her Pony Pals. Lulu Sanders was the Pony Pal who knew the most about wild animals. Her father was a naturalist. He went to faraway places to study animals like elephants and monkeys. Lulu's mother died when Lulu was four years old. After that, Lulu's father took Lulu on his animal trips. She lived in tents, rode elephants, and hid behind bushes to watch the monkeys play.

Lulu loved traveling and studying about animals with her father. When she turned ten, her father decided that Lulu should live in one place for a while. That's when she came to Wiggins to stay with her grandmother.

Lulu thought she'd be bored living in Wiggins. But then she met Anna and Pam and became a Pony Pal. Lulu told Anna that she had more adventures being a Pony Pal than she did traveling with her father.

Anna and Pam Crandal lived in Wiggins all their lives. Of all the Pony Pals, Pam knew the most about ponies and horses. Pam's mother was a riding teacher, and the Crandals had lots of ponies and horses. Pam rode a pony before she could even walk.

Anna and Pam met in kindergarten when Anna showed Pam a drawing she made of a pony. Anna is dyslexic, so reading and writing are difficult for her. But she loves to draw and paint.

Anna held up the drawing she'd made of the black cat.

"That's perfect," said Lulu.

"You're the best artist, Anna," added Pam.

"Thanks," said Anna. "You write the words and I'll draw a cat for the next poster."

Pam printed the words on the first poster.

Lost Cat
Found on Main St. A black male cat.
He is friendly and likes ponies. Call
Crandal Animal Clinic 555·3714.

Soon the three posters were finished.

"Let's ride into town and put them up," said Anna.

The girls went out to the paddock. Anna couldn't wait to see the cute cat again. But the cat wasn't on the fence post next to Acorn anymore.

"I wonder where he went," said Lulu.

"Maybe he was just visiting and now he's gone home," said Pam.

Anna pointed to Acorn's back. "There he is," she giggled.

"Where?" asked Lulu. Then she giggled, too. The cat was sitting on Acorn's back.

"He's the same color as Acorn's mane," said Pam. "No wonder we couldn't see him."

Anna lifted the cat off Acorn.

"Kitty, you can't come to town with us," she told the cat. "You might get hit by a car."

"Let's put him in the animal clinic kennel while we're gone," said Pam. "He'll be safe there."

Pam took the cat from Anna and carried him to the animal clinic. Anna and Lulu brought the ponies to the barn to saddle up.

The Pony Pals rode on Riddle Road, then Mudge Road, and down Main Street. Their first stop was the post office. Anna ran in and pinned the poster to the community bulletin board.

Next, they rode to Upper Main Street. Anna stayed with the ponies, while Pam and Lulu brought a poster into the library.

The last stop was the green market. Pam held the ponies while Anna and Lulu went in. Lulu pinned the poster to the bulletin board.

"I'm going to buy the cat a toy," Anna told Lulu. "You want to help me pick one out?"

"Sure," said Lulu.

Anna led the way to the pet section of the store. There were five different kinds of toys for cats. Anna and Lulu looked them over.

"This one is my favorite," said Anna. She

held it up. A red plastic ball and yellow feather hung from a long piece of wire. Lulu batted the little ball with her finger. A bell tinkled inside the ball.

"He'll have fun with this," said Lulu.

The girls rode back to the Crandals. Anna went to the kennel room to see the cat. She held the toy above his head. He reached up with two paws to try to catch the ball. When the bell rang he jumped back. Then he tried to catch the ball again. Anna tied the toy to the kennel door so the cat could play with it whenever he wanted.

There were six other animals in the clinic. Brandy, the German shepherd, was sound asleep. He had a big bandage around his belly. There were three other cats and two more dogs. Anna knew that their owners were missing them.

Anna lifted the cat out of his kennel and carried him outside. Acorn was standing at the paddock fence near the clinic. When he

15

saw the cat, he whinnied happily. The cat leaped from Anna's arms and ran over to Acorn.

The cat stayed in the paddock with the ponies while the girls went in for dinner. After dinner and dishes, Anna carried the cat back to the kennel for the night. He purred in her arms. It's fun to have a cat, thought Anna.

After she said good night to the cat, Anna went to the barn office. Pam and Lulu had already unrolled the three sleeping bags. The girls sat on their pillows and played cards. At nine-thirty they turned off the lights and got into their sleeping bags. They lay in the dark and talked about the cat and all the cute things he did.

If he was my cat, Anna thought, he'd sleep on my bed. Anna closed her eyes. She fell asleep thinking about Acorn and his new friend.

Suddenly, Anna woke up. She looked at her watch. It was two-thirty in the morning. What woke me up? Anna wondered. She heard pounding hooves and screeching ponies. She jumped out of her sleeping bag.

"Pam, Lulu!" Anna shouted. "Wake up! Something's wrong in the paddock!"

Danger!

The Pony Pals slipped their boots on their bare feet. As they ran out of the office, they grabbed their jackets and put them on over their pajamas. What's happened? wondered Anna. Why are the ponies upset?

"I'll get halters and lead ropes," shouted Pam, as she hurried to the tack room.

Anna and Lulu ran down the barn aisle and outside. It was snowing. The three ponies were running along the fence line.

Their high-pitched whinnies almost sounded like screams.

"None of them looks hurt," said Anna.

Pam ran up beside her friends and handed each of them a halter and lead rope.

When Lightning saw Pam, she stopped running and pawed the ground. Pam went over to her pony. "It's okay," Pam said in a calm voice. "Everything is going to be okay." She slipped the halter over Lightning's head.

Snow White came over to Lulu. The pony snorted, but she let Lulu put on the halter and lead her in a circle.

Pam was leading Lightning around in a circle, too. "This should calm them down," she said.

Acorn was the last pony to stop running. Anna went over to him and put her hand on his neck. She stroked it gently. "What's wrong, Acorn?" she asked. Acorn snorted and shook his head.

"I wish they could tell us what happened," Anna said.

"Maybe a pack of coyotes ran through the paddock," said Lulu. "That could wake up a pony and frighten her."

"And if one pony is upset, it can upset the others," said Pam.

Lulu brushed snowflakes off Snow White's mane. "The snowstorm might have upset Snow White," she said. "She doesn't like snowstorms."

"Let's put them in the new barn for the rest of the night," said Pam. "Some of the stalls are empty."

"Good idea," said Anna. She clipped a lead rope to Acorn's halter.

Pam and Lulu turned their ponies toward the barn. But Acorn didn't want to go.

"You go ahead," Anna told Lulu and Pam. "Acorn is still a little fidgety."

"Okay," said Pam.

"We'll meet you inside," Lulu told Anna.

Pam and Lulu led their ponies to the barn.

Anna's hands felt cold, and the snow was sticking to her eyelashes and hair. She tried to turn Acorn around. "Come on, Acorn," she said. "Snow White and Lightning went inside. It's time to go in." She tried to pull Acorn toward the barn. But he wanted to go in the other direction.

Anna thought, Acorn is being stubborn. I have to be firm with him. "Come on, Acorn!" Anna said sternly. She looked him in the eye so he would know she was serious. But Acorn's eyes didn't have a stubborn look. He looked very upset.

"What's wrong, Acorn?" asked Anna. "Can you show me?"

Anna unclipped the lead rope and let Acorn go free.

Acorn turned quickly and ran across the paddock to the animal clinic. Anna ran after him. I know what's wrong, she thought. Acorn wants to see his cat friend. Anna caught up with Acorn. "Acorn," she said, "you can see the cat tomorrow. Now we're going in the barn."

She tried to grab Acorn's halter. But he turned from her and ran along the fence line next to the clinic. When he stopped, he looked at the clinic and whinnied. Anna finally saw what was upsetting Acorn. Smoke was seeping out of the clinic windows. Through one window of the clinic, Anna saw flickering flames. The clinic was on fire!

Anna turned and ran toward the barn. "Fire! Fire!" she shouted. Acorn whinnied loudly. Anna felt in her jacket pocket and pulled out her whistle. She raised it to her lips and blew the Pony Pal SOS signal.

Lulu and Pam ran out of the barn.

"Fire!" shouted Anna. "In the clinic!"

The two girls ran toward the clinic. "We have to get the animals out!" exclaimed Anna.

"Lulu, call 911!" yelled Pam. "I'll wake up my parents."

Lulu ran back in the barn, and Pam ran toward the Crandals' house.

Anna remembered the sick cats and dogs

that were in the kennel room. She climbed over the fence and ran up to the back door of the clinic.

As she opened the door she heard a dog cough. The cats meowed fearfully. Another dog was whimpering. The air was filling up with smoke. Anna coughed. Through the smoke she could see Brandy. She ran in and opened his kennel door. Brandy jumped out, almost knocking Anna over. Pam was beside Anna now. She grabbed Brandy. "I've got him," she said.

Anna's eyes burned and tears welled up in her eyes. She went to the next cage.

"Pam, take Brandy," shouted a man's voice. "*Do not* come back in here." It was Dr. Crandal. He shouted to Anna. "Get out!"

"But the animals," Anna said with a cough.

Dr. Crandal gave Anna a little push toward the door. "Out!" he shouted.

The smoke burned Anna's throat. What will happen to the animals? she thought. What will happen to the black cat?

Flames

Anna stumbled out of the burning clinic behind Pam and Brandy. She coughed and gasped for fresh air. "But ... all ... the ... animals ..." Anna said breathlessly.

Brandy whimpered. "It's okay," Pam told him. "You're safe now." Pam's mother was there, too. Dr. Crandal handed Mrs. Crandal a cat with a splint on its leg. He ran back into the building.

"Be careful!" Mrs. Crandal yelled to her husband. "Please!"

But Dr. Crandal was already back in

the building. Anna saw flames through Dr. Crandal's office window. The fire was spreading fast.

"Mom, should we take the horses and ponies out of the new barn?" Pam asked. Lulu and Anna exchanged a frightened glance. The fire could spread to the barn. Their ponies were in danger.

Anna remembered that a pony would not leave a burning barn. She'd heard stories of ponies running back into a burning barn after they had been rescued. A pony thought his stall was the safest place to be, even if it was in flames.

Mrs. Crandal looked toward the Crandals' new horse barn. It was right next to the burning clinic. "Yes," said Mrs. Crandal. "Put them in the far paddock. Lulu, you stay and help me with the clinic animals."

"We'll take care of Snow White," Anna told Lulu. "We'll get her out of the barn."

Suddenly, Anna remembered that Acorn wasn't in the barn. He was still outside, near the clinic. Anna's heart stopped beating. Did Acorn jump the fence and go into the burning building? She looked around. It was hard to see anything through the smoke and falling snow. "Where's Acorn?" she asked Pam and Lulu.

"I see him," said Lulu. She pointed to the fence near the clinic. Acorn was pacing back and forth along the fence line. Anna walked over to him.

"It's okay, Acorn," Anna said in a firm voice. She kept talking while she clipped on his lead rope and led him to the far paddock. Pam was walking toward her with Daisy, one of her mom's school ponies.

"We should leave their halters on," Pam told Anna. "In case we have to catch them."

The girls ran into the new barn.

"Take out the horses at the back first," said Pam.

Anna went to the end of the barn and into a stall.

"We're going out to the paddock now, Splash," Anna said in a calm voice. The Appaloosa pony was difficult to handle, but

Anna was firm with him. Splash finally calmed down and Anna led him down the barn aisle and outside.

The sound of fire engine sirens pierced the air. It frightened the ponies. They whinnied and ran up and down the paddock. Pam and Anna were startled, too. But they were glad the firefighters were there. Anna's father was a volunteer firefighter. She hoped that he and the other firefighters could put out the fire before it reached the new barn.

Pam and Anna took out two boarding horses and a school horse. Snow White and Lightning were in the stalls nearest to the door, so they came out last.

A firefighter met them as they left the barn. "Are there any more animals in there?" she asked.

"We got them all out," said Pam.

"Good," the firefighter said. "Don't go back in there, okay?"

"Okay," answered Anna and Pam together.

The firefighter turned and ran back to the fire. Anna saw firefighters spraying the burning clinic with hoses. She thought about the black cat. What if he was still in the clinic?

The horses and ponies were now all safe in the far paddock, although they were confused and frightened by the strange noises and the smell of smoke. Pam and Anna gave them carrots and spoke to them in calm, soothing voices. In a few minutes the ponies and horses finally quieted down.

"Let's help with the clinic animals," said Pam. Anna and Pam climbed over the fence and ran toward the clinic. It was still snowing. The firefighters were hosing down the side of the new barn that was nearest the clinic. Anna heard a firefighter tell Mrs. Crandal, "We've got it under control."

"Where are the animals that were in the clinic?" Pam asked Mrs. Crandal.

"Your dad and Lulu brought them to my office in the old barn," Mrs. Crandal answered.

"Anna, I've been looking all over for you," one of the firefighters said.

It was Anna's father. She hardly recognized him. His face was smudged with smoke and he wore his yellow firefighter's coat. A mask hung around his neck.

"You okay?" he asked.

"I'm fine," Anna answered. "But I have to go check on this cat I found."

Anna gave her father a quick hug. "See you later, Dad," she said.

Pam and Anna ran across the paddock to the old barn. They headed straight to the barn office.

Dr. Crandal was putting a fresh bandage on Brandy's wound. "Pam, please get our two portable folding kennels," he said. "They're in the closet under the hayloft ladder. Anna, could you hold Brandy for a second?"

While Anna held Brandy, she looked around the barn office. The Pony Pals' sleeping bags were piled in a corner. Portable kennels were set up around the

room. The cat with the splint was in one kennel. Two other cats and a dog were in kennels, too. The third dog was lying quietly on top of the pile of sleeping bags. There had been three dogs and four cats in the kennel room that day. Now, Anna counted three dogs and three cats. The black cat was missing.

Anna felt a lump in her throat. What had happened to Acorn's cat? she wondered. Did he die in the fire?

Missing

"Dr. Crandal, did you get all of the animals out of the clinic?" Anna asked nervously.

"Every last one," he said. He smiled at Anna. "Lulu told me that you discovered the fire, Anna. You saved these animals' lives. Thank you."

"Acorn is the one who saved them," said Anna. "He smelled the smoke and led me to it."

"Then you're both heroes," said Dr. Crandal.

Anna looked around the office again. Was

the cat hiding under the desk or asleep on a bookshelf? She still didn't see him. "Where's the black cat that we found this morning?" she said.

Dr. Crandal looked around the office, too. "Isn't he here?" he said.

Lulu came into the office with a bucket of water and empty bowls.

"Where's the black cat?" asked Anna.

"Dr. Crandal got him out of the fire," answered Lulu. "He handed him to me."

"Then what happened?" asked Anna.

Lulu thought for a second. "Brandy started to bleed through his bandage," she said. "I put the cat down so I could help Mrs. Crandal with Brandy. When I looked back, the cat was gone."

Anna felt a shiver run through her. "Do you think the cat ran back into the fire?" she asked Dr. Crandal. "Like horses do?"

Dr. Crandal shook his head. "No," he answered. "I bet he's hiding in one of the barns. That's what a cat would do."

Lulu gave bowls of water to the dogs and

cats. Dr. Crandal and Anna set up kennels for Brandy and the other dog. When the animals were settled, Dr. Crandal and the girls went back outside.

Two of the firefighters were making sure the fire was out for good. "You're lucky, Doc," one of them told Dr. Crandal. "There's a lot of damage to your office. But the flames didn't reach the kennel."

The fire chief came to the doorway of the clinic. "Come on in, Doc," he said. "I'll show you where I think this fire may have started."

Anna and Lulu went to the house. The other firefighters and Mrs. Crandal were having hot chocolate and cookies in the kitchen. Everyone cheered when Anna and Lulu came in. The Pony Pals were heroes. But Anna didn't care about that. She put up her hand to speak.

Everyone was quiet. "Did any of you see a black cat with white paws?" asked Anna.

No one had seen the cat.

After the girls had some hot chocolate

35

and cookies, they went back outside with Mrs. Crandal. It was safe for the horses and ponies to go back in the barn. The girls led the ponies inside, brushed off the snow, dried them off, and put them back in their stalls.

The whole time Anna was helping with the ponies, she kept an eye out for the cat. She didn't see him anywhere. Before Anna left the new barn she gave Acorn an extra treat and a hug. "You're a hero," she told her pony. "You found the fire."

"We have to sleep in my room," Pam told Lulu and Anna. "Mom's office is filled with cats and dogs." Anna didn't care where she slept. She was already looking forward to waking up. Tomorrow she could search for the cat.

Anna was the first Pony Pal to wake up the next morning. She looked out the window. The snow had stopped, but the ground was covered with a thick blanket of soft snow. Anna wondered if the black cat was out somewhere in the cold. She dressed quietly and went out to the new barn.

Anna looked for the cat in the straw and on the rafters of Acorn's stall. The cat wasn't there. Acorn nuzzled Anna's shoulder sleepily. "I'm going to go look for your cat," she told him.

Anna went to the tack room and opened a can of cat food. "Here kitty, kitty," she said. "I have some breakfast for you." The cat didn't appear. Anna looked in the rest of the horse stalls. No cat.

Next, Anna went to the old barn. She checked all the stalls. No cat. She went up to the hayloft and looked behind every bale of hay. No cat. She was coming down the hayloft ladder when Pam and Lulu came into the old barn. "Did you find the cat?" asked Lulu.

"No," said Anna. "He must have run away."

"Maybe he went into the woods," said Lulu.

"It's so cold out there," said Anna. "We have to find him."

Pam put an arm around Anna's shoulders. "We'll all look for the cat," she said. "But first we have to feed our ponies."

"Okay," said Anna.

After the girls fed their ponies they let them out in the paddock. Lightning and Snow White ran happily through the snow. Their hooves kicked up puffs of snow. Acorn ran around the paddock once and then stopped.

Anna was surprised that Acorn didn't run with his friends. Of all the ponies, he liked fresh snow the best. Acorn just stood at the fence and stared into the woods. He's looking for the cat, thought Anna. He misses him.

After they ate breakfast, the girls packed thermoses of hot chocolate and sandwiches. Anna packed a thermos of warm milk for the cat.

"The cat might be hungry," Anna said.

"And cold," Pam added. She put the first

aid kit and an old sweatshirt in her saddle-bag. "This sweatshirt will make a perfect blanket for the cat," she said.

When they went back outside, Acorn was still standing at the fence, looking into the woods. The Pony Pals brought the ponies into the barn and saddled them up for the ride.

"We have important work to do today," Anna told Acorn. "We're going to look for your cat."

Anna put her left foot in the stirrup and swung up on the saddle. Anna was very worried about the cat. Was he injured in the fire? Did he survive the snowstorm? And how could the Pony Pals find a small cat in the big woods?

The Fight

The Pony Pals rode their ponies into the Crandals' big field. They faced more fields and woods. Pam looked around. "Where should we start looking for the cat?" she asked.

"Acorn was staring in the direction of Pony Pal Trail," said Anna.

"Let's start there," said Lulu. "It could be a clue."

The Pony Pals galloped across the field. They slowed down when they came to Pony Pal Trail.

"Look for cat tracks in the snow," said Lulu.

Anna and Acorn took the lead. Anna looked straight ahead for tracks. Lulu looked to the right. And Pam looked to the left.

After a while Pam shouted, "I see some!"

Anna turned Acorn around and looked to where Pam pointed. Small tracks in the snow led into the woods. To Anna, they looked like the tracks a cat would make.

Lulu dismounted to get a closer look at the tracks. She bent over and studied them.

"These are very fresh tracks," she said. "But they have claws. A cat's track doesn't show claws. A fox made these tracks."

Lulu swung back up on Snow White. "Let's keep going," she said.

Anna took the lead again. When they reached the three birches, Acorn stopped. Anna let Acorn's bridle go slack. He sniffed around in the snow.

"Acorn smells something!" said Anna excitedly.

"It's probably something to eat," said Pam. "You know Acorn."

"There could be a clue," said Lulu. "Let's see what he does."

Acorn sniffed for another minute, then he raised his head. He turned toward a trail that started behind the three birch trees.

"Acorn wants to go on the Wiggins Estate," said Lulu.

Ms. Wiggins was a friend of the Pony Pals. She had many wonderful riding trails on her estate. The Pony Pals could ride there whenever they wanted.

Anna rode Acorn onto the Wiggins trail.

Lulu and Pam followed on their ponies.

After a while, Anna saw some tracks in the snow. She brought Acorn up to them. "Look at these, Lulu," Anna called.

Lulu and Snow White trotted up beside Acorn and Anna.

Lulu leaned over and looked at the tracks.

"I can tell from here that they weren't made by a cat," said Lulu. "Those are raccoon tracks."

The girls saw more animal tracks on the Wiggins trails. None of them was made by a cat.

After they had ridden and searched for an hour, Pam said, "Let's give our ponies a rest and some water."

The girls dismounted and led their ponies to Badd Brook. With a stick, Anna broke up the ice along the edge of the water. The ponies lowered their heads and drank.

The wind blew dusts of snow off the pine trees. Some of it fell on the girls. Lulu shivered. "It's cold," she said.

"Let's have our sandwiches and hot chocolate," said Anna. "That will warm us up."

Pam passed out sandwiches and Anna poured hot chocolate. The girls stood near their ponies' warm bodies to eat.

Pam looked up at the sky. "It might snow again."

"We checked the weather forecast before we left," said Anna. "It's supposed to be clear and sunny."

"It's clouding over," said Pam.

"We've had surprise snowstorms before," said Lulu.

Pam looked up at the sky again. "I think we should go back," she said.

"We have to find the cat," said Anna. "If

we go back we're giving up. We can't give up."

"The cat is probably in the barn," said Lulu.

"I looked for him in *both* barns," said Anna. "He's not there."

"Cats can hide in really small places," said Lulu.

"Maybe the fire scared him so he went back to his owner," said Pam. "Maybe he wasn't a stray after all."

Acorn whinnied. Anna put her hand on his head. "Acorn knows the cat is out here," she said. "He wants to keep looking."

"I think we should go back," said Pam. "It's the safe thing to do."

"I agree with Pam," said Lulu. She put her sandwich wrapper and thermos in her saddlebag. "We should go back."

"I thought the Pony Pals didn't give up!" said Anna.

"We're not giving up," said Lulu. "We just don't think the cat is in the woods."

"Anna, it's *two* against one," said Pam.

"Then you two can go back," said Anna angrily. "I'm going to keep looking for the cat." She put out her hand. "Give me the first aid kit. I might need it when I find the cat!"

"You can't stay out here *alone*!" yelled Lulu.

Anna put her hands on her hips. "Oh, yes I can!" she told them. "You can't make me go back."

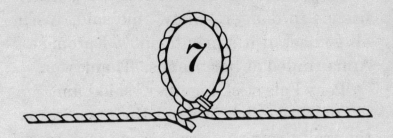

Blood in the Snow

Lulu and Pam exchanged a worried glance. They couldn't make Anna go back with them. But they couldn't leave her in the woods alone either.

Pam sighed. "We'll stay with you," she said.

"Maybe you and Acorn are right," said Lulu. "Maybe the cat is in the woods."

"But promise us you'll turn back if it starts to snow," said Pam.

Anna wanted to find the cat. But she knew it was dangerous to stay in the woods during a snowstorm. She couldn't put her friends in danger. "Okay," she said. "We'll all go back if it starts to snow. I promise." Anna smiled at her friends. "Thank you."

"Pony Pals stick together," said Pam.

The three girls walked their ponies on the trail along the brook. Anna and Acorn led the way.

After a while, Acorn wanted to turn left onto a woodland trail. The girls and the other two ponies followed. They were on the new trail for a few minutes when Anna spotted some fresh tracks in the snow. She was sure they were made by a cat.

"Look over here!" Anna shouted to Lulu and Pam.

Lulu and Pam came over to look.

"See," said Anna. "They don't have claw marks and there are four toes."

Lulu studied the tracks. "You're right,"

she told Anna. "A cat made these. But not a domestic cat. These are the paw prints of a bobcat."

"Bobcats are wild," said Pam.

"Right," said Lulu. She made a circle around a paw print with her riding crop. "See how big they are. They're twice as big as a domestic cat's prints."

"Would a wild cat hunt a domestic cat?" asked Anna.

"I guess," said Lulu. "But bobcats don't go after prey when the snow is deep."

Anna kicked up a puff of snow. "This isn't very deep," she said.

Acorn jerked his head and whinnied. He wanted to leave the trail and go deeper into the woods.

"There's too much brush in there," Anna told Acorn. "You won't fit."

Acorn pulled again. Anna thought, I should be firm with him. Then she remembered that Acorn was a good detective.

"Let's follow Acorn," said Anna. "Maybe he smells the cat."

"If you take off his saddle," said Lulu, "it'll be easier for him to go through the woods."

"I'll stay with Lightning and Snow White," said Pam.

"Thanks," said Anna. "We'll come right back if it starts to snow."

Anna took off Acorn's saddle and bridle. Lulu put the thermos of hot milk, the first aid kit, and an old sweatshirt in her saddle-bag and slung it over her shoulder.

"Okay, Acorn," Anna said. "Show us the way."

Acorn pushed past bushes and brambles and went deep into the woods. Suddenly, he stopped and lowered his head to sniff. Anna and Lulu looked at what he was sniffing.

"These are cat prints!" said Lulu. "And they weren't made by a bobcat! See how small they are. And they're far apart. He was running and leaping when he was here."

"Hurry," said Anna. "Let's follow him."

"Here, kitty, kitty," Anna called as she ran.

Anna saw more cat tracks in the snow, but these were bigger. "Look, bobcat tracks," she told Lulu.

"I hope the bobcat wasn't chasing our cat," said Lulu.

Anna stopped. "Oh, Lulu!" she cried. "He was!" Anna pointed to the ground. The big and small cat prints met and the snow was messed up.

"The bobcat found him," said Lulu sadly. "And they had a fight."

"Maybe the cat got away," Anna said. "Look, the small tracks go over there."

The girls and pony pushed through more bushes to follow the tracks.

"There's blood in the snow," said Lulu.

Anna saw the blood, too. Tears gathered in her eyes.

Lulu stopped and held up a hand. "Listen," she said. "What's that?"

The girls stood still and listened. Anna heard a faint *meow*. "It's a cat," she whispered to Lulu.

Acorn nickered again. "Shush, Acorn," said Anna. "Be quiet."

Acorn nickered again and shook his head. Anna went over to quiet him down. When she reached Acorn, she heard a louder meow.

"I heard it for sure," Anna told Lulu.

"Where?" asked Lulu.

Anna looked all around. There were hundreds of pine branches and bushes for hiding places. It would be hard to see a cat in the dense woods. "I don't see him," she said.

"Here, kitty," said Lulu. "We're here to help you. Where are you?"

The next meow was louder. Acorn looked up at the tree branches above him.

Anna looked up. She saw the cat sitting on one of the highest branches of a tall pine tree. His white paws were red with blood.

Homeless

"There's the cat!" Anna whispered to Lulu. She pointed to the top of the pine tree. "He's on that branch."

Lulu looked up. "I see him," she exclaimed. "He's so high!"

"Here, kitty, kitty," Anna called to the cat.

"Come on down," called Lulu. "We'll take care of you."

The tree branch shook in the wind. The cat held on tight.

"He can't stay there," said Lulu. "He'll fall or freeze to death."

"We have to get him down," said Anna.

"That tree's too high to climb," said Lulu.

Anna put her arm on Acorn's back. "Acorn," she said, "what are we going to do?"

Acorn looked up and nickered at the cat again. He seemed to be saying, "Come on down. You can do it."

The cat crept slowly along the edge of the tree branch. The branch bent with his weight. The cat lost his balance. Anna held her breath as the cat fell through the air. He landed feet first on a lower branch and leaped to the main trunk of the tree. He slid a little and then ran down the tree trunk.

Acorn nickered again and the cat leaped from the tree onto the pony's back.

"Oh, Lulu, he looks awful!" Anna exclaimed. The cat's fur was matted and bloody from the fight with the bobcat. And his ear was split open. A scab ran along the edge of the cut.

Lulu took a closer look at the cut. "I think it stopped bleeding," she said.

"I hope that's all that's wrong with him," said Anna.

"He ran and jumped okay," said Lulu. "So his legs are all right."

"Maybe all that blood is from his ear," said Anna.

"I hope so," said Lulu. "We better get him to Dr. Crandal fast."

Anna took the sweatshirt out of the saddlebag. She wrapped the cat in the sweatshirt and held him in her arms.

"All set?" asked Lulu.

"All set," Anna told Lulu.

Lulu led the way. In a few minutes the two girls, the pony, and the cat were out of the deep woods.

Pam was waiting for them. "You found the cat!" she exclaimed.

"Acorn found him," said Anna.

"Good for you, Acorn," said Pam.

Anna and Lulu told Pam about the cat's fight with the bobcat.

"We shouldn't give him anything to eat or drink until my father sees him,"

said Pam. "In case he has internal injuries."

Pam held the cat while Anna saddled up Acorn. Anna mounted and Pam handed her the cat. After a few minutes of riding, Anna felt the vibration of the cat's purr. "You're going to be okay," Anna told the cat. "We'll get you home as fast as we can." Then Anna remembered. The black cat didn't have a home. "I wish I could keep you," she whispered.

An hour later the Pony Pals were back at the Crandals. They found Dr. Crandal packing up supplies in the damaged animal clinic. "I'm seeing patients in the tack room of the new barn today," he told the girls. "I'll meet you there."

The girls brought the cat to the new barn. Anna put Acorn in a stall while Pam carried the cat into the tack room. Acorn whinnied as if to say, "Hey, where are you taking my cat?"

"We'll bring him right back," Anna told Acorn. She followed Pam into Dr. Crandal's temporary office.

Dr. Crandal carefully opened the sweatshirt and put the cat on the portable examining table. "It looks like this cat has been in a bad fight," he said.

"With a bobcat!" said Anna.

"A bobcat is four times the size of this little fellow," said Dr. Crandal. "Poor cat. He must be bruised and sore." Dr. Crandal felt the cat gently all over. "He doesn't have any big injuries," he said thoughtfully.

Next, Dr. Crandal looked carefully at the cat's torn ear. "This is a nasty bite," he said. "I'll clean it up and give him some antibiotics."

"Can the cat stay in a stall with Acorn tonight?" asked Anna. "I think he'd be afraid in a kennel. After the fire and everything."

"Sure," said Dr. Crandal. "But keep an eye on him." Dr. Crandal wiped the cut ear clean. "Give him warm liquids, then half of a small can of cat food. He can have the rest of the can in a few hours."

"Okay," said Anna. She put her hand out and the cat licked it.

"Acorn and the cat are so cute together," said Lulu.

"Maybe you could keep him," said Dr. Crandal.

"My mom's allergic to cats," said Anna. "I can't have one."

"I can't have a cat either," said Lulu. "My grandmother doesn't like animals. I'm lucky to have Snow White."

"Could we keep the cat here?" Pam asked her father. "Then he could be with Acorn during barn sleepovers. He'd be a Pony Pal cat."

"We aren't adopting any more animals," said Dr. Crandal.

"I know," said Pam. "But this cat is so special."

Dr. Crandal interrupted her. "I see a hundred animals a year that need a good home," he said. "They're all special."

The cat meowed. Dr. Crandal stroked his fur. "You girls bring this cat to St. Francis Animal Shelter tomorrow afternoon. They'll find him a good home." He looked from one girl to the other. "Tomorrow," he repeated. They exchanged a glance. They would have to do what Dr. Crandal told them.

Three Ideas

Anna carried the cat to Acorn's stall and put him on the straw. Acorn happily sniffed him. The cat licked Acorn's nose.

Lulu brought the cat a bowl of warm milk and Anna gave Acorn some grain. Anna watched the cat lap up the milk. "I'm going to miss him," she said sadly.

"They take good care of cats at St. Francis Animal Shelter," said Pam.

"Maybe someone will adopt him," said Lulu.

The cat moved over to a corner of the stall, curled up, and fell to sleep.

"I just wish Acorn and I could adopt him," said Anna. "If only my mom wasn't allergic."

"It's time for a Pony Pal Meeting and three ideas," said Lulu.

"I told my dad we'd help clean up the kennel this afternoon," said Pam.

"Let's all think about this Pony Pal Problem while we're working," said Lulu.

"And we'll have a meeting about it tonight," said Pam.

All afternoon the Pony Pals worked in the kennel room. After dinner they helped Dr. Crandal move the clinic animals from the barn office to the clean kennel room. Finally, at nine o'clock, they laid out their sleeping bags on the barn office floor. They sat on their pillows and faced one another.

"This is a Pony Pal Meeting about keeping the cat for Anna and Acorn," said Pam. "Who wants to go first?"

"I do," said Lulu. She took a piece of paper out of her pocket and read her idea out loud.

The cat can be an outdoor cat. If he doesn't go in the house, he won't make Anna's mother sneeze.

"That's a great idea," said Pam. "Our cats don't come in the house. They live in the barn. We feed them and they have a warm place to sleep."

"But our pony shed isn't very warm," said Anna. "It only has three sides. One side is open."

"I didn't think of that," said Lulu with a frown.

Anna smiled. "I did," she said. She opened up a piece of drawing paper and handed it to Pam. Lulu and Pam looked at Anna's drawing.

"We could build him a little house," explained Anna. "And put a pillow in it. That will keep him warm."

"Good idea," said Lulu. "If it's *really* cold, maybe he can stay in your father's carpentry shop. Your mother never goes there."

"My dad likes cats," said Anna. "And he's not allergic to them."

"What's your idea?" Lulu asked Pam. Pam handed Lulu a piece of paper. Lulu read Pam's idea out loud.

Mice have been getting into Snow White's and Acorn's feed. Tell Mrs. Harley that the cat will keep the mice away.

"I bet the cat would be a good mouser," said Anna. "Lulu and I already saw him chase a mouse from the shed."

"Let's go see your mother first thing in the morning," said Lulu.

"Okay," said Anna. But she still didn't think her mother would let her keep the cat. She remembered how her parents didn't even want her to have a pony. They were afraid that Acorn would take up too much of her homework time. Now she was going to ask them to let her have another pet. One that made her mother sneeze.

Anna wondered if the Pony Pals' ideas were good enough to solve her problem.

The next morning the girls saddled up their ponies and rode to Off-Main Diner.

Since Anna's mother owned the diner, the Pony Pals knew that they would find her there.

The Pony Pals tied their ponies to the hitching post outside the diner and went in. Mrs. Harley was busy with customers. She gave a little wave and said hi. Anna knew it wasn't the right time to ask her mother if she could have a cat.

Anna went to the kitchen to order three pancake specials. Lulu set the table. Pam poured them all milk. Mrs. Harley was still busy with customers. The Pony Pals were almost finished with breakfast when Mrs. Harley finally came over to their booth.

"It's been a busy morning," she said. "But I can take a break until someone else comes in."

Anna moved over so her mother could sit next to her. Mrs. Harley gave her daughter a hug. "I hear Acorn discovered the fire at your place, Pam. He's a hero."

"He is," said Lulu.

"What else have you girls been up to?" asked Mrs. Harley.

"Remember the cat we found, Mom," said Anna. "That we made the posters for?"

"Did anyone claim him?" asked Mrs. Harley.

"No," said Lulu. "And he ran away during the fire."

"But Acorn found him," added Pam. "He's a great cat."

Mrs. Harley sneezed. "I'm so allergic to cats that sometimes I sneeze just thinking about them," she said. "Let's talk about something else." She sneezed again.

The Pony Pals exchanged a glance. How could they ask Anna's mother to let Anna have the cat if they couldn't even talk about him?

Acorn's Shadow

A man and woman came into the diner. Mrs. Harley slid out of the booth and stood up. "Back to work," she said. She went over to her customers.

"We just saw the cutest thing!" the man said to Mrs. Harley.

"There are three darling ponies out front," said the woman. "And one of them has a cat on his back." She pointed out the front window of the diner. "See," she said.

The Pony Pals exchanged a glance. They were all thinking the same thing. The cat must have followed them to the diner. They ran to the window. The black cat was lying across Acorn's shoulders.

Mrs. Harley looked out the window, too. "My goodness," she said. "That *is* cute."

"I didn't know a pony and cat could be such good friends," said the man.

"Whose pony is it?" asked the woman.

"It's my pony," said Anna. "He saved the cat's life."

Pam told them about the bobcat fight and how Acorn found the cat. Mrs. Harley led the customers to an empty booth and gave them menus.

The Pony Pals cleared the dirty dishes from their table. "I'm cutting up a new tray of brownies," Mrs. Harley told the Pony Pals. "You girls can have the broken pieces."

"Thanks," the Pony Pals said together.

Mrs. Harley went behind the counter to

cut the brownies. The girls sat on the stools in front of her.

"I see why you girls were so excited about that cat," said Mrs. Harley. "It's very cute how he plays with Acorn."

"Ask her," Pam whispered to Anna.

"Mom," said Anna. "I was wondering if the cat could stay with us."

"He could live in the shed and never come into the house," said Lulu.

"He'd be an outdoor cat," said Pam. "We'd build him a special house."

"And he's a great mouser," added Anna. "We've been having a lot of trouble with mice in the feed."

"And he would *never* be in the house?" Mrs. Harley asked. "Can you promise me that, Anna?"

"I promise," said Anna.

"Well, then," said Mrs. Harley with a smile.

"Can we keep him, Mom?" asked Anna excitedly. "Really?"

"It looks like he already is Acorn's cat," said her mother.

"Thanks, Mom," said Anna as she gave her mom a big hug.

"So what's the cat's name?" asked her mother.

The Pony Pals exchanged a glance.

"We don't know his name," said Pam.

"We'll have to make one up," said Lulu.

"Let's go make his house and give him a name right now," said Anna.

The Pony Pals ran outside. Anna gave Acorn a big hug. "This cat is yours," she said. "He's your very own cat!"

The girls mounted their ponies and rode on Belgo Road to Main Street. The cat ran beside them. When they reached Main Street they turned left and rode to the Harleys'.

"How about Fuzzy?" said Pam as they dismounted.

"He's not very fuzzy," said Anna.

When the Pony Pals reached the Harleys', they dismounted and took off their ponies' tacks. The cat stayed close to Acorn the whole time.

"We can make the cat's house in my dad's shop," said Anna.

The Pony Pals went to Mr. Harley's workshop in the garage.

Anna loved woodworking. She learned to build things by helping out her father. "Let's make the house two feet square," she said. "Pam, you find some wood and I'll do the drawing."

Pam took a measuring tape from the workbench and went over to the pile of scrap wood in the corner of the shop.

"We could call the cat Black Beauty," said Lulu. "That's a perfect name for a beautiful black cat who is best friends with a pony."

"Black Beauty is too long for a little cat," said Anna.

As the girls built the house for the cat, they tried out other names. But they couldn't come up with a name they all liked.

"We could just keep calling him Kitty," said Lulu.

Anna and Pam didn't think that was a good idea.

"Maybe we should just call him No Name," said Pam.

"No," said Anna and Lulu together.

Anna hammered the roof onto the little house. "We'll think of something," she said.

The Pony Pals carried the cat's house out to the shed. They put it on top of the feed bin. Anna looked around the yard. "Now, where's that cat?" she asked.

Pam pointed. "Look," she said. "He's over there. Right in Acorn's shadow. He's following him everywhere."

"He *is* Acorn's shadow," said Lulu with a giggle. "He goes everywhere Acorn goes."

"That's it!" exclaimed Anna.

"What?" asked Pam and Lulu together.

"Shadow. It's a perfect name for Acorn's cat," said Anna.

"Shadow," repeated Pam. "I like it."

"Me, too," said Lulu.

The Pony Pals raised their hands to hit high fives. "All *right!*" they shouted.

Acorn whinnied. And Shadow jumped up on his back. The Pony Pals burst into laughter. Acorn had his own cat.

Dear Reader:

I am having a lot of fun researching and writing books about the Pony Pals. I've met many interesting kids and adults who love ponies. And I've visited some wonderful ponies at homes, farms, and riding schools.

Before writing Pony Pals I wrote fourteen novels for children and young adults. Four of these were honored by Children's Choice Awards.

I live in Sharon, Connecticut, with my husband, Lee, and our dog, Willie. Our daughter is all grown up and has her own apartment in New York City.

Besides writing novels I like to draw, paint, garden, and swim. I didn't have a pony when I was growing up, but I have always loved them and dreamt about riding. Now I take riding lessons on a horse named Saz.

I like reading and writing about ponies as much as I do riding. Which proves to me that you don't have to ride a pony to love them. And you certainly don't need a pony to be a Pony Pal.

Happy Reading,

Jeanne Betancourt

Pony Pals

Do you love ponies?

Be a Pony Pal®!

**Anna, Pam, and Lulu want you to join them
on adventures with their favorite ponies!**

**Order now and you get a free pony portrait bookmark and two
collecting cards in all the books—for you *and* your pony pal!**

❏ BBC48583-0	#1	I Want a Pony	$2.99
❏ BBC48584-9	#2	A Pony for Keeps	$2.99
❏ BBC48585-7	#3	A Pony in Trouble	$2.99
❏ BBC48586-5	#4	Give Me Back My Pony	$2.99
❏ BBC25244-5	#5	Pony to the Rescue	$2.99
❏ BBC25245-3	#6	Too Many Ponies	$2.99
❏ BBC54338-5	#7	Runaway Pony	$2.99
❏ BBC54339-3	#8	Good-bye Pony	$2.99
❏ BBC62974-3	#9	The Wild Pony	$2.99
❏ BBC62975-1	#10	Don't Hurt My Pony	$2.99
❏ BBC86597-8	#11	Circus Pony	$2.99
❏ BBC86598-6	#12	Keep Out, Pony!	$2.99
❏ BBC86600-1	#13	The Girl Who Hated Ponies	$2.99
❏ BBC86601-X	#14	Pony-Sitters	$3.50
❏ BBC86632-X	#15	The Blind Pony	$3.50
❏ BBC74210-8		Pony Pals Super Special #1:The Baby Pony	$5.99

Available wherever you buy books, or use this order form.

Send orders to Scholastic Inc., P.O. Box 7500, 2931 East McCarty Street, Jefferson City, MO 65102

Please send me the books I have checked above. I am enclosing $_____ (please add $2.00 to cover shipping and handling). Send check or money order — no cash or C.O.D.s please.

Please allow four to six weeks for delivery. Offer good in the U.S.A. only. Sorry, mail orders are not available to residents in Canada. Prices subject to change.

Name_____ Birthdate ____/____/____

       First   Last   M   D   Y

Address_____

City_____ State_____ Zip_____

Telephone (_____)_____ ❏ Boy   ❏ Girl

Where did you buy this book? ❏ Bookstore ❏ Book Fair ❏ Book Club ❏ Other

What do Frankenstein, Bigfoot, and Santa Claus have in common?

They're all a part of the creepy, weird, wacky and funny things that happen to the Bailey School Kids!™ Collect and read them all!

☐ BAS43411-X	#1	Vampires Don't Wear Polka Dots	$2.99
☐ BAS44061-6	#2	Werewolves Don't Go to Summer Camp	$2.99
☐ BAS44477-8	#3	Santa Claus Doesn't Mop Floors	$2.99
☐ BAS44822-6	#4	Leprechauns Don't Play Basketball	$2.99
☐ BAS45854-X	#5	Ghosts Don't Eat Potato Chips	$2.99
☐ BAS47071-X	#6	Frankenstein Doesn't Plant Petunias	$2.99
☐ BAS47070-1	#7	Aliens Don't Wear Braces	$2.99
☐ BAS47297-6	#8	Genies Don't Ride Bicycles	$2.99
☐ BAS47298-4	#9	Pirates Don't Wear Pink Sunglasses	$2.99
☐ BAS48112-6	#10	Witches Don't Do Backflips	$2.99
☐ BAS48113-4	#11	Skeletons Don't Play Tubas	$2.99
☐ BAS48114-2	#12	Cupid Doesn't Flip Hamburgers	$2.99
☐ BAS48115-0	#13	Gremlins Don't Chew Bubble Gum	$2.99
☐ BAS22635-5	#14	Monsters Don't Scuba Dive	$2.99
☐ BAS22636-3	#15	Zombies Don't Play Soccer	$2.99
☐ BAS22638-X	#16	Dracula Doesn't Drink Lemonade	$2.99
☐ BAS22637-1	#17	Elves Don't Wear Hard Hats	$2.99
☐ BAS50960-8	#18	Martians Don't Take Temperatures	$2.99
☐ BAS50961-6	#19	Gargoyles Don't Drive School Buses	$2.99
☐ BAS50962-4	#20	Wizards Don't Need Computers	$2.99
☐ BAS22639-8	#21	Mummies Don't Coach Softball	$2.99
☐ BAS84886-0	#22	Cyclops Doesn't Roller-Skate	$2.99
☐ BAS84902-6	#23	Angels Don't Know Karate	$2.99
☐ BAS84904-2	#24	Dragons Don't Cook Pizza	$2.99
☐ BAS84905-0	#25	Bigfoot Doesn't Square Dance	$3.50
☐ BAS84906-9	#26	Mermaids Don't Run Track	$3.50
☐ BAS88134-5		Bailey School Kids Super Special #1: Mrs. Jeepers Is Missing!	$4.99

Available wherever you buy books, or use this order form

Scholastic Inc., P.O. Box 7502, 2931 East McCarty Street, Jefferson City, MO 65102

Please send me the books I have checked above. I am enclosing $_____ (please add $2.00 to cover shipping and handling). Send check or money order — no cash or C.O.D.s please.

Name _____

Address _____

City_____ State/Zip _____

Please allow four to six weeks for delivery. Offer good in the U.S. only. Sorry, mail orders are not available to residents of Canada. Prices subject to change.

BSK1096